Where's the Elephant?

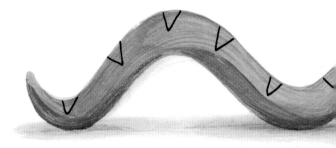

Where's the **Parrot?**

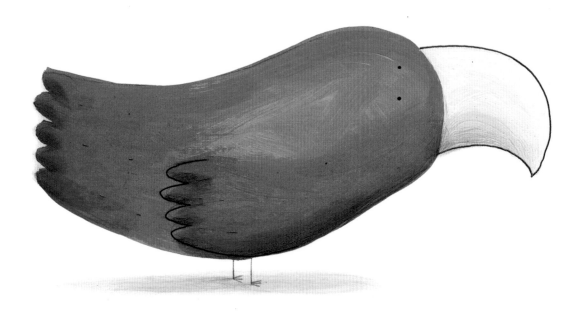

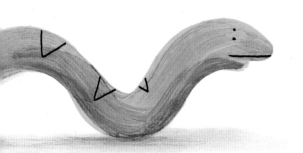

Where's the **Snake?**

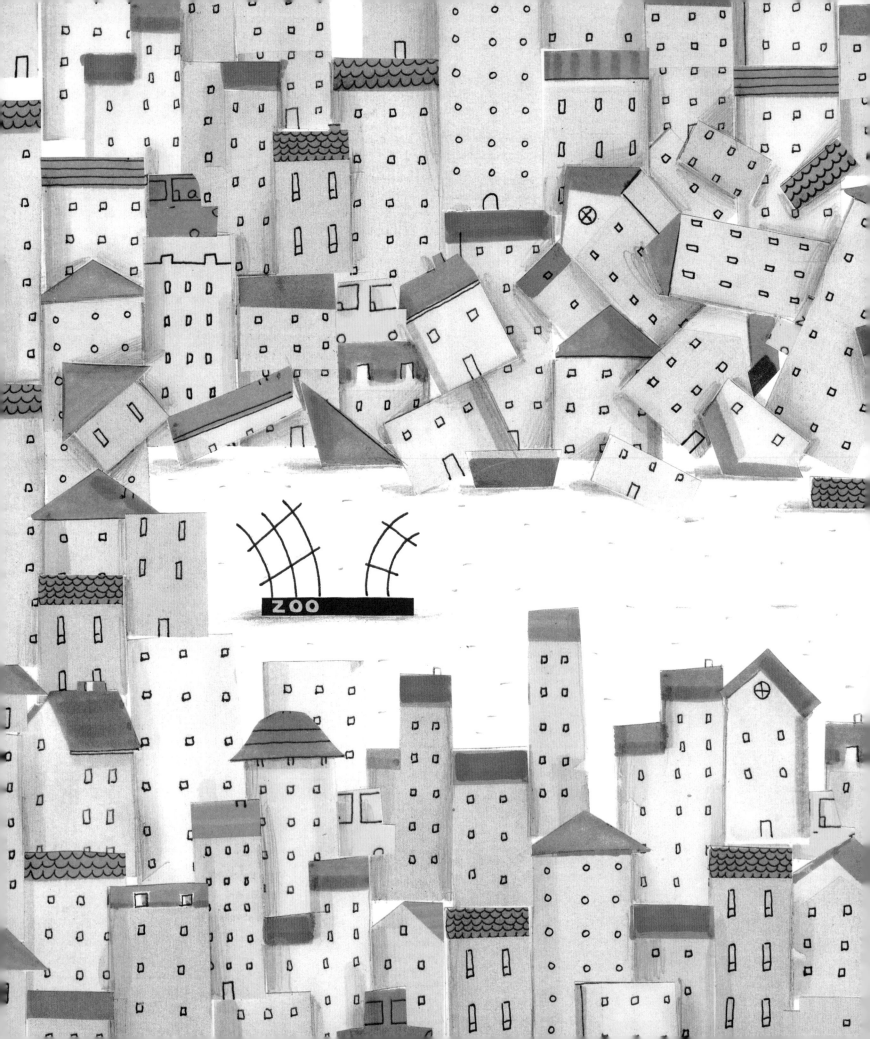

THE STORY BEHIND THIS BOOK

When I visited Brazil five years ago, I saw parts
of the Amazon Rainforest set on fire to clear the
way for soybean production.

Since then I have searched for an idea to talk about
deforestation, but it wasn't until two years ago,
at the Edinburgh Book Festival, that I found my
inspiration – *Where's Wally?* Suddenly everything
was clear in my mind and I started the first sketches . . .

Barroux

EGMONT
We bring stories to life

First published in Great Britain 2015
by Egmont UK Limited
The Yellow Building, 1 Nicholas Road, London W11 4AN
www.egmont.co.uk

Text and illustrations copyright © Barroux 2015
Barroux has asserted his moral rights.

ISBN 978 1 4052 7648 1 (hardback)
ISBN 978 1 4052 7138 7 (paperback)

A CIP catalogue record for this book is available from the British Library.

FSC
www.fsc.org
MIX
Paper from
responsible sources
FSC® C018306